PRAISE FOR *WE WALKED ON*

"With beautiful writing, Chehade masterfully creates the sense of living with a civil war that uses a city as its battleground — how enmities build, how the violence becomes both terrifying and commonplace, how life stops and starts and the ordinary continues, but with everything coloured by war."

—Kamila Shamsie, author of *Home Fire*, winner of the Women's Prize for Fiction 2018

"A moving book that details, with tenderness and intimacy, the lives fractured and uprooted by the Lebanese Civil War. Writing intelligently, Thérèse Soukar Chehade maps the 'siphoning of the soul' caused by religious and class divides fomented by colonial powers—divides that remain urgently relevant today—and the toll of these ruptures on those who survive. The story has a slow-burn quality that pulls the reader deep into the world of the boisterous, diverse communities of Beirut who grow and separate together, focusing especially on Rita, a Convent student who, even in her youth, begins to yearn for the rebellious, fun-loving teenager that she once was, and Hisham, a teacher devoted to his students and family, who writes in stealth about the war. Most of all, *We Walked On* is an ode to those who anchor us in kindness in times of grief and irrecoverable loss: teachers, mentors, friends, and the writers who reignite in the consciousness of the living, who must now tell their own stories, true and fierce."

—Uzma Aslam Khan, author of *The Miraculous True History of Nomi Ali*, a *New York Times*' pick for Best Historical Fiction 2022 and winner of the 2023 Massachusetts Book Award in Fiction.

"*We Walked On* is a treasure, paean to longing and celebratir life amidst the rubble and desp Soukar Chehade has crafted a n

fear, and genuine hope despite the fever of 'animal terror,' where a brief snowfall invites dancing in the street, the vanished return in dreams, and books offer refuge from total annihilation. *We Walked On* is a novel of rare talent and exquisite intimacy—a crucial, lyrical exploration of survival."

—Margot Douaihy, author of *Scorched Grace*, a *New York Times Book Review* Editors' Choice

"With tremulously gorgeous prose and an unsparing yet compassionate gaze, Thérèse Soukar Chehade draws us deep into a dazzling world lost to war. The Beirut of these pages feels both shockingly immediate and achingly distant, and its denizens vibrate with aliveness. I sunk into this intricate novel, into its sumptuous pleasures and deep sorrows, and I was changed by it."

—Debra Jo Immergut, author of *You Again* and *The Captives*

"With lush, atmospheric prose, Thérèse Soukar Chehade recreates a time of beauty before civil war and the bewilderment of the subsequent slide into chaos and devastation. Her sensitive and keen eye allows us to enter the scene and feel the simple pleasure of a paper cone of peanuts, the everyday vexations of family tensions, and then with a single deft image—a soldier goes by in an open car and you remember him chasing his little sister on the playground—to feel the impossibility of reconciling the past with the present. *We Walked On* finds the universal in the individual, gives us the aching beauty of everyday things, and an affecting reminder that a place is not lost that exists in memory."

—Kate Southwood, author of *Falling to Earth* and *Evensong*

"If the title *Being There* were not already taken, it would have worked admirably for Thérèse Soukar Chehade's harrowing and poignant story of two people trapped in the Lebanese Civil War of the mid-1970s. In recounting the intertwined experiences of a 14-year-old girl named Rita and Hisham, the literature